ENGINE NUMBER SEVEN

ELEANOR CLYMER
ENGINE NUMBER SEVEN
Illustrations by Robert Quackenbush

Holt, Rinehart and Winston
New York ❀ Chicago ❀ San Francisco

Library of Congress Cataloging in Publication Data

Clymer, Eleanor Lowenton, date
  Engine number seven.

    SUMMARY: In a little town in Maine the old narrow gauge
railroad is gradually replaced by cars, trucks, and buses that do
the same job just as well—or can they?
  [1. Maine—Fiction. 2. Railroads—Trains—Fiction]
I. Quackenbush, Robert M., ill. II. Title.
PZ7.C6272En   [Fic]   74-20911
ISBN 0-03-013701-2

This book is for Alison

☼ *Foreword*

The Two-Foot Railroads of Maine

Fifty years ago, the state of Maine was crisscrossed by a network of railroad tracks. They were only two feet wide, much narrower than regular tracks, and the trains that ran on them were tiny, much smaller than regular trains. Some people called them Lilliputs. There have been narrow-gauge trains in other states, but none had as many as Maine.

The idea came from a man named George Mansfield. In the 1870s — a hundred years ago — he traveled in Wales. There he saw little trains running over the mountains down to the seacoast, carrying slate from the slate quarries. He thought they would be just right to carry lumber, stone, and slate — and people — over the hills and valleys and around the lakes of Maine.

The little railroads were much cheaper to build than bigger ones. For the short distances between towns they were perfect, and in the depths of winter when snow covered the roads, the little trains went where nothing else could go.

One town after another wanted a railroad line, and the idea and the tracks spread all over the state. For fifty years, children grew up knowing and loving the little trains, and wishing they could have them to play with.

Then, in the 1920s, the Lilliput railroads began to die out. Cars and trucks took over, automobile roads were built, and the trains weren't making enough money to stay in business. One by one, the engines were sold for scrap, the cars were broken up, and the tracks rusted away. By 1935 they were gone.

Engine Number Seven is a story about such a train. It didn't really happen just that way, but it could have happened.

A few of the little trains of Maine are still in existence. That is because they have been saved and put into museums. Some of those museums are out of doors, and you can still go for a ride on one of the little two-footers, hear its whistle toot, and see the smoke trail back from its chimney.

But if you can't do that, perhaps you can ride on a regular train. We still have trains, and I hope we always will.

Eleanor Clymer
Katonah, New York
February 1975

❀ *Chapter One*

Up north in the state of Maine, where the summer sun is hot and the winter snows are deep, there was a small village named Hogus.

Hogus had some white houses, a church, a general store, a hotel for summer people, and a one-room school. It also had a train.

It was a very small train. It ran on a track only two feet wide. It had an engine with a tender for coal, and two cars. One was a passenger car with red plush seats and a stove for cold days. The other car was for mail and freight. On the front and sides of the engine, the number 7 was painted in gold.

Mr. Hobbs was the engineer. He ran the train.

Mr. Griggs was the fireman. He shoveled the coal and rang the bell.

Mr. Wooley was the conductor. He sold the tickets, swept the cars, and gave the signal for starting the train.

Twice every day Number Seven chugged down to Winslow, twenty miles away. She carried potatoes and blueberries and eggs that the farmers brought in their wagons. She brought back mail and groceries, and everything else that people needed in Hogus.

This was back in the days when not many people had cars. And in Hogus there were hardly any.

Anybody who wanted to go shopping in Winslow, or visit their aunts or cousins, could take the train in the morning and come back in the afternoon. When the summer people got tired of sitting on the porch, they could always go for a train ride. People who were going to Boston changed at Winslow to the regular train, which looked like a monster beside little Number Seven. Summer or winter, she never missed a trip.

Everybody in Hogus loved Number Seven. But especially Dot and Sam.

Dot lived across the street from the train

station. Mr. Hobbs was her grandpa. She didn't know which she loved more, Grandpa or Number Seven. She said she was going to be an engineer like him when she grew up.

For her birthday she asked for overalls and a trainman's jacket, and her grandpa added an engineer's cap like his own.

Dot's best friend was Sam Beatty. Mrs. Beatty, who ran the hotel, was his mother.

"I'll be a fireman when I grow up," he said. "I'll shovel the coal and ring the bell."

But that was a long way off. Meanwhile, every chance they got, they went down to the train yard to help take care of Number Seven.

Mr. Hobbs explained how the engine worked. You made a fire in the firebox. That heated the water and made steam. The steam pushed the rods that made the wheels go. He showed them how to oil the rods and wheels so they went smoothly.

Mr. Wooley let them punch holes in the used tickets. And on Saturdays Mr. Griggs let them ride in the cab and pull the bell cord, and see the flames in the firebox, and wave to the children who came down to the track to watch the train go past.

They were so busy that they didn't notice that things were changing in Hogus.

It was Mr. Bodger who started the changes. Besides owning the store, he was also the first selectman on the town council.

One day after school, Dot and Sam were on their way to see Number Seven start on her afternoon trip. In front of Mr. Bodger's store, they saw a red truck. Mr. Bodger was unloading boxes from it. A few people were watching, and Dot and Sam went over to look too.

"Is that yours, Mr. Bodger?" Sam asked.

"Yes, it is," said Mr. Bodger. "Now I don't have to wait around for the train. I can just drive down to Winslow and bring every- thing back myself. That's the way to get things done. Get in, and I'll take you for a lit- tle ride."

Dot and Sam got in, and off they went. But they didn't like it. It smelled of gasoline, and they both got carsick. They were glad to get down.

"I like the train better," said Dot.

"Me too," said Sam.

A number of people agreed with them. But others thought having your own truck was a good idea. Some of the farmers decided to get trucks to bring in their vegetables. However, there was no gasoline pump in Hogus. They had to go all the way to Winslow for gas, so they did their shopping there instead of at Mr. Bodger's store. He began to lose trade.

"Serves him right," said Mr. Hobbs.

But it wasn't long before Mr. Bodger did something about it. One day, there was a shiny red gas pump in front of his store.

"Now, folks, you can get your gas right here," he said. "This is the way to get things done."

Mr. Bodger had more trade than ever. But old Number Seven had less. Soon she was making only one trip a day, to carry the mail and a few passengers.

In the afternoon, when Dot and Sam went down to the train shed, Mr. Hobbs would be sitting on a bench and would hardly talk to them.

"Grandpa's been awfully cross lately," Dot said.

Then one evening Mr. Bodger called a town meeting. Everybody came to find out what it was about. Mr. Bodger pounded the table and said, "The meeting will come to order."

Everybody kept quiet.

"Friends," said Mr. Bodger, looking very important, "I'm here to get things done. Times are changing. Now, lots of people in

this town have cars or trucks. Why do we need to spend money to keep up the railroad?"

"He's right," some people said.

"Will somebody make a motion to close down the railroad?" Mr. Bodger asked.

"I so move," said Mr. Huggins, the postmaster.

"Second the motion," said one of the farmers.

"All in favor say aye!" There was a shout of "Aye!"

"All opposed say no."

Five voices said, "No." Mr. Hobbs, Mr. Griggs, Mr. Wooley, Dot, and Sam. Dot and Sam didn't count, because they were too young to vote. But they could still talk.

"What about Number Seven?" Dot asked.

"Are you going to sell her?" Sam demanded.

"We might as well sell her for junk," Mr. Bodger said.

"No!" shouted Mr. Hobbs. "You'll never do that. I'll buy her myself."

And he got up and stamped out of the hall. Dot and Sam ran after him. They walked down to the train yard. The moon shone down on Number Seven where she stood waiting on the track for the next day's run.

"Grandpa," said Dot. "I'm glad you're going to buy her. But what will you do with her?"

That's the trouble," said Mr. Hobbs, sadly. "I don't rightly know."

There really wasn't anything to be done with Number Seven. A few days later, Mr. Hobbs ran the little train into the shed. And there she stayed.

Mr. Griggs got a job in Mr. Bodger's store. Mr. Wooley got a job in the post office.

Mr. Hobbs worked in his garden. Or he sat on the porch and smoked his pipe. If people stopped to say it was a nice day, he growled, "What's nice about it?"

"Grandpa's awfully cross," said Dot.

"I wish we could do something," said Sam. But there didn't seem to be anything to do.

☼ Chapter Two

Summer came. It was the time for swimming and berry-picking, fishing and picnicking. Then suddenly, summer was almost over.

One day, on the way to the pond with their bathing suits wrapped in their towels, Dot and Sam passed the railroad yard. Morning glory vines climbed up the shed walls. Grass and goldenrod grew between the tracks.

Dot said, "Too bad Number Seven's not running. It would be a good day for a train ride."

She was remembering how it used to be with the little train standing, shining and

ready, on her track, the wheels freshly oiled and a plume of smoke rising from her smoke-stack.

Sam said, "Let's go inside and see her."

The big doors were locked, but there was a loose board around in back. They squeezed in.

There stood Number Seven, all alone in the shed. Dusty streaks of sunlight shone down from cracks in the roof.

Dot climbed up into the cab. Spider webs got in her hair. A bird flew out from some-where. Bits of dried mud from wasps' nests lay on the floor. The iron was rusty and the brass dull.

The bell cord hung down. Sam reached up to give it a pull, but Dot grabbed his arm. "Sh!" she whispered.

Someone was coming in. The door opened with a creak. They heard voices. Mr. Bodger was talking to Mr. Hobbs.

"Be reasonable, Hobbs," he said. "Times are changing. You can't keep this old wreck here forever."

"Don't you call Number Seven a wreck!" Mr. Hobbs shouted. "I'll keep her as long as I like. She's mine."

"But the shed belongs to the town," said Mr. Bodger. "And the town needs it. You've

got to get that train out of here. And that pile of coal too. People elected me to get things done."

And he marched out. Mr. Hobbs stood muttering to himself.

Dot put her head out of the cab window. "Hello, Grandpa," she said. "Hi, Mr. Hobbs," said Sam.

"What are you doing there?" Mr. Hobbs demanded. "Come down from there, the both of you."

"We heard Mr. Bodger," said Dot. "What did he mean? Why should you get Number Seven out?"

"It's the town's shed," said Mr. Hobbs.

"But why?" Dot asked.

"They're building a new school halfway to Winslow—a big school. All you kids from miles around are going to it. The town is getting a bus, and they want the shed to keep the bus in. How do you like that?"

"I won't go," said Dot.

"You have to go," said Mr. Hobbs. "It's the law."

"But what about Number Seven?"

Mr. Hobbs shook his head. "I reckon it's the end of the line. I'll have to sell her for scrap." He took out his red handkerchief and blew his nose. "Nobody wants her," he said.

"We want her," Sam shouted. "We won't let her go."

Mr. Hobbs said sadly, "There's no place to keep her."

Dot looked at her grandpa, sadly stuffing his handkerchief back in his pocket. She looked at Number Seven, standing idle and dusty. She thought how awful it would be to see the little engine dragged away to be cut up by blowtorches. She couldn't stand it. There had to be a way out. Suddenly she had an idea.

"Grandpa!" she said. "You know that siding down by the lake where they used to keep extra cars?"

"Ayuh!" said Mr. Hobbs. "I know it. What about it?"

"If we could get Number Seven down there, she could stay there. That wouldn't bother anybody. Then at least we wouldn't have to sell her for scrap iron."

"But the track belongs to the town," said Mr. Hobbs. "Mr. Bodger wants to sell the right-of-way."

"Maybe it won't matter," said Sam, "as long as they can use the shed."

But Mr. Hobbs shook his head again. "How are we going to get her down there?"

"Grandpa!" said Dot. "Let's clean her up

and run her one more time. We'll have one more ride on her. We'll blow the whistle and Sam can ring the bell. Come on, Grandpa!"

"It's a lot of work to get an engine ready to run," said Mr. Hobbs.

"We'll help," said Sam. "We've only got a little while till school starts but we'll come after school."

Mr. Hobbs began to look more cheerful. "It's against the law," he said. "I suppose you know that. You need a permit to run an engine. And I don't have one anymore."

"Will they put us in jail, Grandpa?" Dot asked.

Mr. Hobbs chuckled. "We'll try it and see," he said.

"Let's start right now," said Dot.

"All right. You kids start on the cars while I take a look at the engine. And shut that door. We don't want the whole town to know what we're doing."

Dot and Sam climbed into the passenger car. The mice had chewed holes in the plush seats. Spiders had spun their webs over the windows.

"This is a mess," said Dot. "I'll go and get some rags and a broom."

She ran home and snatched an armful of rags, a broom, and a mop.

"Where are you going with those things?" her mother asked. It was strange to see Dot interested in housework.

"I'm helping Grandpa clean up Number Seven," said Dot.

"I thought you were going swimming," her mother said.

"This is more important," said Dot.

They brushed away the mouse nests and the cobwebs. They swept the floor. By suppertime the car looked much better. There were still the windows to wash and the woodwork to polish. They decided to do that next day.

Then they started on the engine. That was harder.

They had to take off the side plates and put in sheets of asbestos. It was a good thing Mr. Hobbs had some extra supplies put away. It was also good that Number Seven was so little, or they could never have done it.

They put in new flues. They cleaned out the boiler. Sam climbed up and looked down the smoke pipe. Grandpa said that sometimes birds built their nests in there. Sure enough there was one. It had to be poked out with a broom handle.

They cleaned the rust off the wheels and the driving rods.

"If a rod breaks, the train will stop," said Mr. Hobbs. "And if a tire breaks it may make a hole in the boiler."

They oiled everything. They tested the water tank and filled it. They painted the engine black, and polished the brass till it shone like gold.

There was a lot of work to do, and it took a long time.

One day Mr. Bodger came over. "Well, Hobbs," he said, "what's going on here? I thought you were going to get that train out. The bus is coming tomorrow. We've got to get things done."

Mr. Hobbs climbed down from the engine. "I'm working on her," he said. "When she's ready to roll, I'll get her out."

"I see you're cleaning her up," said Mr. Bodger. "You're not doing that just to sell her for scrap."

"Don't seem that way," said Mr. Hobbs. And not another word would he say. Mr. Bodger was puzzled. He went back to his store.

Then the big yellow bus arrived. As there was no shed for it, it stood in Mr.

Bodger's yard. Mr. Griggs got the job of driving it.

A few days later the new school opened. Mr. Griggs drove the Hogus children to school in the morning. Then he went home. In the afternoon he went back to get them. In between, he sat by the stove and kept his feet warm.

For it was getting colder. Much colder.

"Looks like we'll have an early winter," said the old folks. "Squirrels are burying lots of nuts. Geese flew south early. They know."

Mr. Bodger laid in plenty of high boots and snow shovels. He was ready.

The farmers got in hay and feed for the animals. Everybody split up plenty of stove wood. It was too early for winter, but it surely felt like it.

One afternoon, when Dot and Sam got back from school, they saw a crowd of people in front of Mr. Bodger's store. They were looking at a big yellow machine. Mr. Hobbs was there too.

"What is it?" Dot whispered.

"Ask him," said her grandpa, pointing to Mr. Bodger.

"It's a snowplow," said Mr. Bodger, proudly. "The latest thing. It's to clear the road so the school bus can go through."

"Where are you going to keep it?" Mr. Hobbs asked.

"That's a good question," said Mr. Bodger. "We're a-going to keep it in the shed, right next to the school bus. And that brings me to the next matter, which is, that you have till Friday to get that there train out of there. The train *and* that pile of coal. That's my last word."

Mr. Hobbs walked back to the train shed. Dot and Sam hurried after him.

"What'll we do, Grandpa?" Dot asked.

"Got to get her out," said Mr. Hobbs. "Today is Wednesday. Tomorrow morning I'll fire her up. Tomorrow afternoon after school we'll run her out. The pile of coal will have to set there."

Dot and Sam ran home. They could hardly wait for Thursday afternoon.

Chapter Three

2078368

Thursday morning the sky was gray. It was cold. Dot and Sam shivered as they walked to the bus and climbed on board.

"Number Seven has a nice stove," said Sam. "Why can't they have a stove on the bus?"

That reminded Dot of Grandpa working in the train shed, getting Number Seven ready for her last trip. Suddenly she jumped up.

"I forgot something," she said. "I have to go back." She jumped off the bus.

"We're leaving! You'll be late!" Sam yelled. But Dot was running to the train shed.

Grinding its gears, the bus started off without her.

Dot ran to the shed. Mr. Hobbs was working on the coal pile, shoveling coal into the tender.

"What are you doing here?" he asked.

"I came to help you," said Dot, grabbing another shovel.

"You'll get your dress dirty," said Grandpa.

"Who cares?" said Dot, shoveling coal into a bucket.

"All right," said Grandpa. "Let's get the fire going."

Then he looked out through the open door. It was snowing. Clouds of snowflakes filled the air.

"Great day in the morning!" said Mr. Hobbs.

It snowed all morning, while Mr. Hobbs and Dot worked in the shed. They shoveled more coal. They put water in the boiler and sand in the sand dome.

At lunchtime they went home to Grandpa's house for some hot soup. Mr. Hobbs turned on the radio.

A voice said, "Travelers' warnings are in effect. An unexpected storm has dumped inches of snow in two hours. Schools are closing early."

"That's good," said Dot. "Then Sam will get his ride. I was afraid we'd have to go without him."

Her grandpa shook his head. "I don't think we're going anywhere," he said. "Not today."

"But Grandpa! We have to get her out of there. We have to get her to the siding."

"And how are we going to get back from the siding? Fly?"

"I never thought of that," said Dot. She turned off the radio.

In the silence, another noise was heard. A grinding, growling noise. They looked out of the window. Mr. Griggs was trying to get the school bus started. It wouldn't move. It was snowed in!

Mr. Hobbs pulled on his coat and cap and ran out. Dot ran after him. Mr. Bodger came running out of his store. He jumped into the seat of the snowplow. He turned the key.

"Pretty low on gas," he said, peering at the dashboard. He backed the plow up to the gas pump. He jumped out and stuck the nozzle into the gas tank of the plow. Nothing happened.

"What's the matter, Bodger?" Mr. Hobbs asked. "Won't your newfangled gadget work?"

"Tank's out of gas," said Mr. Bodger. "Reckon all those farmers filled up their trucks yesterday. Now I'm empty."

Mr. Wooley came out of the post office.

"Get shovels," Mr. Bodger yelled. "Shovel the road so the school bus can get started."

Some more people came out.

"Don't just stand there," Mr. Bodger screamed. "We've got to get things done!"

"Calm down, now, Bodger," said Mr. Wooley. "We can't shovel the road all the way to Winslow. This here storm has got the whole county tied up."

But some of the mothers spoke up. "Who's going to fetch the kids?" Mrs. Beatty demanded.

"That's right," said another. "You got them there, now you bring them home."

"Can't bring them home without a snow-plow, ma'am," said Mr. Griggs.

Dot pulled her grandpa's sleeve. "I know where there's a snowplow," she said. "And we don't need gas to run it."

"You're right, Dot," said Mr. Hobbs. "Come on. Griggs, you come too."

They ran to the train shed. In a corner lay Number Seven's plow. Mr. Hobbs started to drag it out, but it was too heavy for him.

"What are you doing?" Mr. Griggs demanded. "Have you gone crazy?"

"Griggs, just keep still and make yourself useful," said Mr. Hobbs. "Get up there and get some steam going. Then help me with this plow."

Mr. Griggs shoveled madly. Then he jumped off and helped Mr. Hobbs hitch the snowplow on the engine. Then all three of them climbed on board.

"Now, Dot!" shouted Mr. Hobbs. "Ring the bell!"

Dot pulled the cord. "Clang-clang! Clang-clang!"

There were shouts from outside. People came running.

"What's going on? Where's the fire?"

Mr. Hobbs opened the throttle. Chug-chug! went the wheels.

"Wait for me!" shouted Mr. Wooley. He ran into the shed, grabbed his conductor's hat, stuck it on his head, and leaped aboard. Out of the shed chugged old Number Seven, with Dot pulling the bell cord and Mr. Hobbs blowing the whistle.

"Whoooo! Whoooo! Who-whoooo!"

Mr. Bodger came charging across the road.

"Where do you think you're going, Hobbs?" he asked.

"Going to get the kids," said Grandpa.

"You got no permit to operate a train!" shouted Mr. Bodger.

"We'll discuss that later," Mr. Hobbs called back. "First we got to get things done!"

Number Seven was on her way, her plow throwing out a great curve of snow, her little chimney and sand dome just showing over the snowbanks, and a ribbon of smoke trailing after her and mixing with the whirling snowflakes.

"Whoooo! Whoooo! Who-whoooo!" she whistled at the crossings.

People ran out of their houses, astonished to see Number Seven once more. They waved and shouted, and the crew waved back.

On the steps of the schoolhouse, the Hogus children waited for the bus. But no bus came for them. The other buses had come and gone.

"How are we going to get home?" the Hogus children asked.

Then, through the dusk and the drifting

snow, they heard a bell and saw the light of a head lamp, coming slowly along the track that ran past the school. Teachers and children stared as if they were seeing a ghost. The only one who understood was Sam.

"It's Number Seven!" he yelled. "She came for us!"

"Hooray!" everybody cheered. They ran through the deep snow, and climbed on board.

"Hi, Mr. Wooley! Hi, Mr. Griggs! Hi, Mr. Hobbs! Hi, Dot!" they called joyfully.

Mr. Wooley leaned far out and waved his arm. Mr. Hobbs, watching, nodded. Then slowly, carefully, Number Seven backed all the way home to Hogus.

At the station, she chugged to a stop. The people came running to snatch the children who jumped down, shouting happily, "We had a train ride!"

But Mr. Bodger was not so happy. He came striding through the snow. His face was red — maybe from the cold. Mr. Hobbs climbed down. His face was red too, perhaps from the heat of the engine.

"Well, Bodger," Mr. Hobbs said, "I guess I broke the law. I ran the train without a permit, and I trespassed on private property, and maybe a few other things."

Mr. Bodger said, "Yes, you did, but I'll overlook it this time."

"*You'll* overlook it!" shouted Mr. Hobbs. "Who got these kids home?"

"You can't carry kids without a permit," said Mr. Bodger.

"You mean it's better to leave them there in the snow?" yelled Mr. Hobbs.

The two men were getting madder and madder. In a minute they might even get into a fight. Some of the other people were getting into arguments.

Sam's mother scolded Mr. Griggs. "You've got no right to run a bus if you can't drive in snow."

Dot's mother said, "Our own schoolhouse was good enough. Why do we need a new one?"

Dot and Sam looked at each other. "Wait!" Dot called, but nobody heard her. She had to do something. But what?

"Sam!" she said. "Now's your chance. Climb up there and ring that bell."

"You bet!" said Sam. Like a monkey he scrambled up into the cab, with Dot after him.

"Clang-clang!" went the bell.

There was instant quiet. Dot leaned out of the cab and shouted, "I want to speak."

The grown-ups stared at her in surprise. Mr. Bodger looked annoyed. "Come down from there, little girl," he said. "Don't interrupt."

But Mr. Hobbs said, "Let her talk."

"Okay," said Mr. Bodger, "but make it quick. We've got things to do."

"I just want to say," said Dot, "that Number Seven got us home. But who's going to get us to school tomorrow?"

"That's a good question," said Mr. Griggs. "We've got no gas, the plow won't work, and the bus can't make it."

"Let's stay home!" said the children.

"Nothing doing!" said their mothers.

"It's a fact," said Mr. Wooley. "That's only the first snow. We've got the whole winter ahead of us. We need the train."

"And what about in summer?" Mrs. Beatty asked. "The summer people like it too."

Mr. Bodger looked at the crowd. It seemed he was outnumbered.

"All right, folks," he said. "The will of the people shall prevail. Tomorrow night, we'll have a town meeting."

"No!" the people shouted. "Let's have it right now."

"Okay," said Mr. Bodger. "We'll have it now."

It was the queerest town meeting that ever was held. Standing on the platform, with the snow twinkling down, Mr. Bodger called out, "Will someone make a motion?"

Mrs. Beatty answered, "Cars are all right but we need a train too. I move we keep Number Seven."

"I second the motion," said Mr. Griggs.

"All in favor say aye!" said Mr. Bodger.

"Aye!" came the shouted reply.

"All against." There was no sound but the hissing of snow on the engine.

"The motion is carried," said Mr. Bodger.

Dot, leaning down from the cab, grinned at her grandpa. He gave her a big wink.

"That's the way to get things done," he said.

❋ About The Author

Eleanor Clymer was born in New York City and grew up there, but now lives in a small country village. She enjoys photography, travel, and digging into the past.

Driving around the countryside, she found here and there the abandoned tracks of railroad lines that once carried people and goods from place to place. From this came the idea for ENGINE NUMBER SEVEN.

Mrs. Clymer has written forty-eight books for young people. Among them are: *My Brother Stevie, How I Went Shopping and What I Got* and *Luke Was There. Engine Number Seven* is book number forty-nine.

❋ About The Artist

Robert Quackenbush was born in California and brought up in Arizona. He is a graduate of the Art Center College of Design in Los Angeles, and since 1956 has been a painter, teacher, and illustrator in New York City.

He has illustrated over sixty books for children and adults for which he has received honors and citations from the Society of Illustrators and the American Institute of Graphic Arts. In addition, his art has been exhibited at leading museums throughout the country.

❋ About The Book

The text is Photo Century Schoolbook. The display type is Chisel. The artist has illustrated the book with scratchboard technique.